For William and Timothy
    – J.S.

For Nina, with love
    – T.W.

ISBN 0-590-63596-4

Text copyright © 1996 by Julie Sykes.
Illustrations copyright © 1996 by Tim Warnes.
All rights reserved. Published by Scholastic Inc., 555 Broadway, New York, NY 10012, by arrangement with Little Tiger Press.

12 11 10 9 8 7 6 5 4 3 2 1   8 9/9 0 1 2 3/0

Printed in the U.S.A.   08
First Scholastic printing, September 1998

Shhh!

by **Julie Sykes**

Pictures by **Tim Warnes**

Scholastic Inc.

New York Toronto London Auckland Sydney

It was Christmas Eve,
and Santa was feeling jolly.

"Jingle bells,
Jingle bells,
Jingle all the way!" sang Santa noisily
as he loaded the toys into the sleigh.
"Shhh, Santa," whispered the reindeer.
"You have to be quiet tonight or
you'll wake the children!"
"I'll try to," said Santa. "But I *do* like singing."

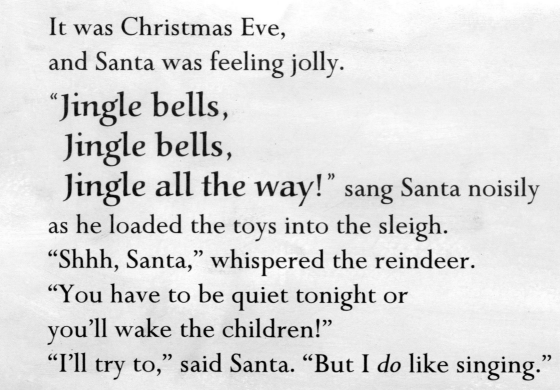

NORTH POLE

Over the earth they flew
toward the first house.

Santa was so excited that he forgot
to land on the roof and ended up
in the front yard instead!

"DEAR ME,
DEAR ME,
DEAR ME!" roared Santa, spying a friendly
cat. "Merry Christmas, Cat! Do you think
they'll mind if I use the back door?"
The cat waved her tail in the air.
"Shhh, Santa," she whispered. "They won't mind,
but you mustn't wake the children!"
    "Of course I won't," said Santa,
        jumping out of the sleigh.

Santa threw the sack of presents over his shoulder and tiptoed along the garden path. The house was silent, and everyone was asleep except for a snowman in the yard.

"OOH,
OOH,
OOH, OOPS!" cried Santa,
sliding on a patch of ice and crashing
to the ground.

"Shhh, Santa," whispered the snowman.
"You mustn't wake the children!"
"Sorry," said Santa, picking up his presents
and bouncing indoors. "But Christmas *is*
my favorite time of year!"

When he reached the Christmas tree,
Santa stopped bouncing and pulled some
presents out of his sack.

One was a jack-in-the-box, which burst open.
Santa jumped in surprise.

"HEE, HEE,
HEE, HEE,
HEE, HEE, HEE!"
laughed Santa,
clapping his hands.
"Shhh, Santa," whispered
the family's dog.
"You mustn't wake the children!"

"No, we mustn't wake the children," agreed Santa. He put his finger to his lips and crept toward the fireplace to fill the stockings.

But he didn't notice the
tinsel on the floor
until it was too late . . .
Santa tripped and went

BUMPITY,
BUMPITY,
BUMP! across the room,
landing on a roller skate.
Toys flew everywhere as he
skidded across the carpet and
fell headfirst into the fireplace.

"AAH,
AAH,
ACHOO!" sneezed Santa,
rubbing the soot from his nose.
"Shhh, Santa," said the kitten
sleepily from an armchair by the hearth.
"You mustn't wake the children!"
　　　　　"Yes, we must be quiet," whispered
　　　　　Santa, scrambling to his feet.

Santa picked up his sack and hurried back to his sleigh, for there were many more places to go before Christmas Day.
Finally, they visited the last house, and Santa's sack was empty.

Santa rubbed his eyes sleepily and called,
"Home, Reindeer!"
And with a toss of their heads and a jingle
of bells, the reindeer leapt into the sky.

"**HO, HO, HO!**" shouted Santa loudly.

"Here we are, home at last!"

" I know, I know," he added softly.

"We mustn't wake the children!"

It had been a busy night,
and Santa felt very tired.
He made himself a cup of hot cocoa,
put on his slippers, lay back in his armchair,
and fell fast asleep . . .

". . . Z Z Z Z," snored Santa.
"MUNCH, MUNCH, MUNCH!" crunched the reindeer as they ate their supper.
"Shhh!" squeaked Santa's little mouse.

"YOU MUSTN'T WAKE SANTA!"